Ruby's Dinnertime

Paul and Emma Rogers

little 🌳 ORCHARD

Another one for Ruby - with love

Rogers, Paul, 19

Ruby's
dinnertime /
Paul and Emma
          JPIC

1586903

Orchard Books
96 Leonard Street, London EC2A 4XD
Orchard Books Australia
Unit 31/56 O'Riordan Street, Alexandria, NSW 2015
First published in Great Britain in 2002
ISBN 1 84121 666 6
Text © Paul Rogers 2002
Illustrations © Emma Rogers 2002
The rights of Paul Rogers to be identified as the author and
Emma Rogers to be identified as the illustrator have been
asserted by them in accordance with the
Copyright, Designs and Patents Act, 1988.
A CIP catalogue record for this book is available from the British Library
1 3 5 7 9 10 8 6 4 2
Printed in Singapore

Ruby's got a special chair,

With a table
of its own.

When she eats, she looks just like
A queen upon her throne.

Ruby likes bananas.

And ice-cream's
such a treat.

She simply loves spaghetti -
To play with, not to eat!

Ruby's got a special cup.

It's got a
little spout,

So when you shake it in the air
Not all of it comes out.

She's got a
special bowl as well,
That sticks onto the tray.

You have to tug
it really hard,

Before
it comes
away.

She's even got a fork and spoon -

Just right for playing her drum.

"Dinnertime!" calls Mummy.

But Ruby
doesn't come.

She sometimes takes an apple,

And biscuits from the shelf.

She plays at teddies' picnic,

Then eats it all herself.

But Ruby's not been playing
At picnicking today.

Daddy goes to
bring her in.

Ruby runs away!

"Not come in!" shouts Ruby,

"Want to stay out there!"

Daddy carries Ruby in,
And sits her on
the chair.

Mummy picks the spoon up
And scoops some carrot on.

She lifts the spoon to Ruby's mouth -
But Ruby's mouth has gone.

"Come along,"
says Mummy.
"Try to eat
some more."

"Ruby finished!"
Ruby says,
And flings it
on the floor.

"Dear, oh dear," says Daddy.
"What's all this about?

Eat up now,
like rabbit."

Ruby spits it out!

Ruby tugs her bib off.
She pulls her chair away.

Whatever is she up to?
Ruby doesn't say.

She goes to get
a cushion,

A grown-up plate and cup,

"Have dinner now!"
says Ruby,

And eats the whole lot up!